Jeanne Willis

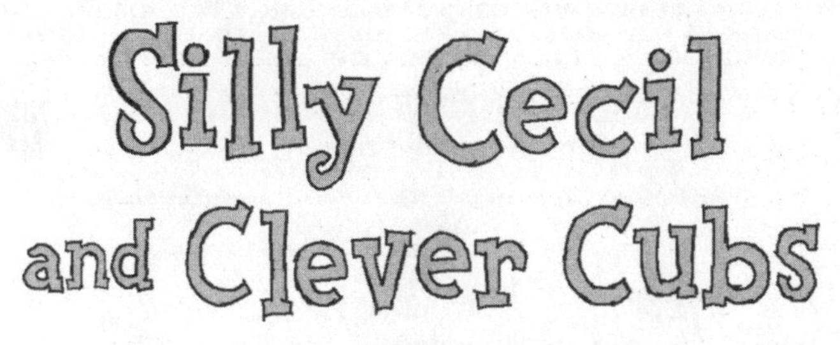

Illustrated by
Mike Terry

PUFFIN BOOKS

Published by the Penguin Group
Penguin Books Ltd, 80 Strand, London WC2R 0RL, England
Penguin Group (USA) Inc., 375 Hudson Street, New York, New York 10014, USA
Penguin Group (Canada), 90 Eglinton Avenue East, Suite 700, Toronto, Ontario, Canada M4P 2Y3
(a division of Pearson Penguin Canada Inc.)
Penguin Ireland, 25 St Stephen's Green, Dublin 2, Ireland (a division of Penguin Books Ltd)
Penguin Group (Australia), 250 Camberwell Road, Camberwell, Victoria 3124, Australia
(a division of Pearson Australia Group Pty Ltd)
Penguin Books India Pvt Ltd, 11 Community Centre, Panchsheel Park, New Delhi – 110 017, India
Penguin Group (NZ), 67 Apollo Drive, Rosedale, North Shore 0632, New Zealand
(a division of Pearson New Zealand Ltd)
Penguin Books (South Africa) (Pty) Ltd, 24 Sturdee Avenue, Rosebank,
Johannesburg 2196, South Africa

Penguin Books Ltd, Registered Offices: 80 Strand, London WC2R 0RL, England

puffinbooks.com

First published 2010
1

Set in Adobe Caslon 14.75/28.5pt
Typeset by Ellipsis Books Limited, Glasgow
Made and printed in England by Clays Ltd, St Ives plc

British Library Cataloguing in Publication Data
A CIP catalogue record for this book is available from the British Library

ISBN: 978-0-141-32885-0

www.greenpenguin.co.uk

Contents

I

Cecil was one of those pompous pedigree cats who didn't see an animal when he looked in the mirror. What he saw was a person trapped in a furry suit and hat who just happened to have a tail.

It was his greatest wish to slip into some silk jodhpurs, saddle up a pony and gallop around the grounds of Futtock Mansion, yelling 'yahoo!' just like Young Master Hooray, the pompous pedigree boy who also lived there.

Cecil wanted to be like Young Master Hooray so much he even wore his riding boots when he thought no one was looking. Unfortunately they came up to his armpits and no matter how hard he practised walking up and down he was fooling nobody. Least of all Cubby, the scruffy

little tabby who had strayed into the kitchen a few weeks back and refused to leave.

'Cecil, you don't look nuffin' like the Young Master,' he said. 'You look like a fat old cat who's fallen into a pair of wellies and can't get out.'

'I'd watch your step if I were you, Mr Cubs,' snapped Cecil as he slipped and did the splits trying to kick the boots off. 'It wouldn't pay to rub me up the wrong way. The only reason I allow you to stay here is because I'm a gentleman.'

'Silly me,' said Cubby, 'I thought it s because you were too feeble to fight me off, but all along it was because you're a gent! Only I'd never have guessed, what with the way you keep threatening me with Master Hooray's spud gun – that's not very gentlemanly, is it?'

'You wouldn't recognize a true gentleman if he kicked you up the backside with a hand-stitched slipper!' exploded Cecil. 'Yet I only have to look at you to know you were born in the gutter. No doubt your father was a pickpocket and your mother was an alley cat.'

None of this was true. Cubby's dad might have come from the wrong side of town and his mum may have belonged to a lady who sold knickers at the market, but he wasn't born in a gutter – he was born in a box of woolly pants under the knicker stall and very comfortable it was too.

Unfortunately the Knicker Lady could barely afford to feed him, his mother and his fifteen brothers and sisters. She hardly sold any knickers because the kittens had torn them and made them all furry, so Cubby was constantly on the lookout for food.

If he hadn't been so hungry, he'd never have sneaked into Mrs Dortmunder's shopping trolley, stuffed himself with the sausages at the bottom and fallen fast asleep. When he finally woke up, he found himself on the other side of town being unpacked along with the groceries in a very posh kitchen, and in the kitchen was a very posh cat asleep in a very posh wicker basket – it was Cecil.

Mrs Dortmunder – who was the Hoorays' housekeeper – was somewhat surprised to see Cubby sitting there with bits of sausage hanging off his whiskers, but she wasn't half as surprised as Cecil and not nearly as cross.

Cecil was so cross he pinned back his ears and puffed himself up until he spilled over the edge of his basket like a snowy owl that had outgrown its nest. At that moment, the elastic on his sapphire-studded collar snapped with a loud ping, scattering the gems through the air.

'Wotcha, mate, you all right?' Cubby said, helping himself to Cecil's favourite Russian caviar, which had been served in a solid gold saucer.

'Who the fuzzy heck are you?' shrieked Cecil, jabbing the air with his paws as if they were chubby boxing gloves. 'Did I hire you? No, I don't think so. You can't just come waltzing in here and eat another cat's caviar. Now get out before I fetch Young

Master Hooray's spud gun . . . Don't just stand there looking gormless, Mrs Dortmunder! Chop those potatoes into pellets!'

Of course, Mrs Dortmunder could not understand a word Cecil said and, even if she had, she wouldn't have taken any notice. She wasn't impressed by airs and graces, and was not about to be told what to do by the likes of an overgrown pedigree cat.

Having put the groceries away, Mrs Dortmunder struggled into her industrial decontamination suit and pottered off with a bucket of bleach, a blow torch and a gas mask to give Young Master Hooray's bedroom a thorough blitzing while he was at boarding school.

Cecil officially belonged to Young Master Hooray who'd had him since he was a kitten. He'd been a gift for his fifth birthday and for some years Master Hooray happily believed that Cecil was the polar-bear cub he'd ordered his mother to buy for him.

But when Cecil refused to grow to the required size and shape of such a bear, Young Master Hooray began to wonder if what he'd actually got was a miniature variety that happened to say *miaow* instead of *grrrr* because it was so small.

To test this theory, he waited until winter and took Cecil for a swim in the frozen carp lake. It was only when Cecil showed no signs of enjoying the icy water whatsoever that Master Hooray realized that he was no polar bear and that his ghastly, cruel parents had fobbed him off with a fluffy, fat white cat. It was a very expensive cat but, even so, it was not what he'd asked for at all. Master Hooray was deeply disappointed and, forever after, Cecil felt so guilty about being completely the wrong species he went out of his way to please him.

Young Master Hooray loved being the boss of Cecil and, for some strange reason, Cecil thought it was an honour to be used by him as a hot water bottle, a foot rest, a hand towel or a tea tray. He worshipped the lad and though it was obvious to everyone else that he was a mad, spoilt, stuck-up little boy, Cecil couldn't see it. His only regret was that Master Hooray spent so much time away.

'Just you wait until he gets back from boarding school, Mr Cubs!' screeched Cecil. 'He's a frightfully good shot. One word from me and you won't know what's hit you! Run along . . . Shoo!'

But Young Master Hooray wasn't due home until Easter and Cubby – who was afraid of nothing and nobody – was going nowhere. He knew which side his bread was buttered, and at Futtock Mansion they had the best bread, the best butter, the best of everything.

If he stayed here, he would no longer have to eat the fish guts and chicken gizzards that the market traders dropped, nor raid the litter bins for half-eaten kebabs. He could dine on pheasant and quail instead. Stuffed skylarks in jelly! He could drink double cream and champagne. He could lie on a silk pillow stuffed with the hair of baby

angels and fall asleep in front of a roaring log fire, just like Cecil.

But he was nothing like Cecil and their differences became more obvious with every passing day. They were opposites in almost every way: Cecil's whiskers were long and droopy; Cubby's were short and curly. Cecil's nose was pink and shiny; Cubby's was covered in stains. Cecil's tummy looked like a woolly football; Cubby's was so flat it looked as if Mrs Dortmunder had pressed it with her steam iron.

It wasn't just their looks that set them apart – it was their likes and dislikes. Cecil liked to study the newspaper, but Cubby preferred to pee on it. Cecil liked to listen to classical music while Cubby preferred a good old sing-song round the piano.

But the thing that caused the biggest arguments was which programme to watch on telly and it was this that finally made the fur fly.

It happened the week before Young Master Hooray was due home. His frightfully rich parents had gone to Scotland to visit the queen, and Mrs Dortmunder had been instructed to pop into Futtock Mansion twice a day to feed Cecil and freshen up his jewel-encrusted litter tray.

The parents knew nothing of Cubby and no doubt they would throw him out if they caught him, so he had to do a lot of sneaking around. Luckily, Futtock Mansion was huge, so it wasn't hard for a little cat to make himself invisible, secretly sleeping on the canopy over a four-poster bed, or camouflaged on a tapestry pouffe, or lounging in the linen cupboard.

The only person who *did* know about Cubby was Mrs Dortmunder. She had a very soft spot for him – which is why she didn't push him off the sofa and switch off the television the day all hell broke loose. Instead, she left him where he was, watching his favourite cartoon in peace.

The peace didn't last long. As soon as Mrs Dortmunder had closed the front door behind her, in came Cecil. He snorted at Cubby, then plonked himself down on the remote control and changed the channel with his bottom cheek.

'I was watching that,' sighed Cubby.

'Not any more!' boomed Cecil. 'It's my mansion and my television and I'm not watching that rubbish. I like a bit of culture in the afternoon.'

Cubby yawned. He didn't like a bit of culture at any time of day and this programme looked as if it might be extremely boring. It was about something called 'reincarnation', which he'd never heard of, presented by a man with a long grey beard called Professor Birtwhistle.

Just as Cubby suspected, the show was as dull as a wet weekend. But, as it really was a wet weekend and he didn't fancy going out in the rain, he stayed where he was and tried to amuse himself by interrupting Cecil, who'd insisted that he called him 'Sir'.

'Sir Cecil, what is reincarnation? Is

it a sort of flower? Only when I lived with the Knicker Lady there was a flower stall next to hers which sold carnations. Luvverly red ones there were, and pink ones, and yellow ones . . .'

'Do shut up,' grumbled Cecil.

'Orange ones . . . blue ones. Get your luvverly carnations, two pound a bunch.'

Cecil glared at him. 'If you *listened*, instead of carrying on like a street seller, you would know that reincarnation isn't a flower. It's the belief that when we die we come back to life as someone else.'

'Like who, Sir Cecil?' asked Cubby, rather hoping he'd come back as a tiger.

Cecil turned up the volume.

'If you listen to Professor Birtwhistle, instead of pulling the tassels off that cushion, you might find out,' he groaned.

Cubby did as he was told. According to the professor, when someone died, who or what they came back as in the next life depended on how they'd behaved before. If they'd been bad, they might be reincarnated as a weed or a worm. If they'd been good, they might come back as something

better, such as a kangaroo or a king. But Cubby wasn't convinced.

'This is boring,' he said. 'Can I watch the footy now?'

For a moment, Cecil couldn't speak – he was far too excited. Ever since he was a kitten, he'd dreamed of being human so he could be like Young Master Hooray. He'd thought he was stuck with being a cat forever, but now Professor Birtwhistle had given him an idea. Cecil had got it into his fluffy head that as he was such a perfect cat, if he died tomorrow, he was bound to come back as a perfect gentleman or possibly a prince. He could hardly wait to be reincarnated.

'Mr Cubs,' he said, slapping his podgy thigh, 'I should like you to kill me!'

2

Cecil might have been pompous and rather mean, but Cubby didn't have the heart to kill him, no matter how much he begged.

'Mr Cubs, as your superior, I insist you kill me. I wish to be reincarnated into a person in order to go hunting, shooting and fishing with Young Master

Hooray, and nothing you can say or do will change my mind.'

Cubby lifted his paw above his ear and set about washing his boy-bits with gusto.

Cecil stared, aghast. '*Meeugh!* That's exactly the kind of revolting behaviour that makes me not want to be a cat!' he wailed. 'People use a flannel and soap.'

Cubby stopped licking himself and looked up. 'I bet Master Hooray doesn't,' he said. 'If the smell in his room is anything to go by, that boy hasn't had a bath in living memory.'

'Nonsense,' insisted Cecil, 'he's very fragrant.'

If the truth be told, Young Master Hooray smelled like a farmyard on a hot day, but Cecil had very little sense of smell because he had cake crumbs permanently up his nostrils. Cubby knew it was pointless arguing with Cecil and sauntered off.

'Mr Cubs . . . *Mr* Cubs! Come back and kill me this second, do you hear?' boomed Cecil. 'We can go out into the garden, I'll close my eyes and you can sink your fangs into my throat and leave me to suffocate in the pansies – I shan't mind.'

'I wouldn't waste my time,' said Cubby. 'Let's face it, you ain't coming back as a squire or even a slug, sir. Once you're brown bread, that's it.'

'Brown bread?' muttered Cecil. 'Are you seriously suggesting I'll come back as a wholemeal loaf?'

'No, no, brown bread is cockney rhyming slang for "dead", sir,' explained

Cubby. 'I don't think you'll come back as anything, not even a crusty white roll. It won't work.'

'And who are you to argue with Professor Birtwhistle?' sneered Cecil. 'He's a very well-educated man. I believe that he went to the same boarding school as Young Master Hooray. Have you even been to school, Mr Cubs?'

'I've been to more schools than you've had hot dinners,' said Cubby proudly. 'I got meself some luvverly grub from the food bins there.'

'But you didn't get yourself an education,' sighed Cecil, 'which is why you can't begin to understand something as complicated as reincarnation, but I can, because I sit in on Young Master Hooray's homework sessions.'

'You sit *on* his homework, more like,' said Cubby.

'Ah, but it's the *way* I sit,' insisted Cecil. 'Do you know, Mr Cubs, I feel sorry for you. You've been deprived of a decent education, so I'm going to teach you a lesson.'

Cubby – who in many ways knew a whole lot more about life than Cecil – escaped into the conservatory, but Cecil followed him in.

'I shall prove to you that reincarnation exists if it's the last thing I do, Mr Cubs!'

Cubby climbed into a potted palm, dug a hole in the soil and squatted over it.

'Must you do that there?' Cecil winced. 'Bring on the day when I am a person and I can sit on the lavatory, like Master Hooray.'

'Better out than in,' said Cubby, straining. 'Won't be a sec. Mrs Dortmunder's prune and pigeon pie always goes straight through me.'

Cecil clutched his nose while Cubby cheerfully buried what he'd done, scattering dirt and gravel to all four corners of the room.

'Phew, that's better,' Cubby said. 'What were you saying before, mate?'

Cecil, who hated being called 'mate', rolled his eyes. 'It's *Sir* Cecil to you. And I was saying, before I was so rudely interr–'

'Yes, Sir Cecil, sir!' interrupted Cubby. 'What were you Ceciling? I mean saying?'

Cecil gritted his fangs.

'With the aid of a dead mouse, I am going to conduct a scientific experiment to prove my theory of reincarnation,' said Cecil just before lunchtime. 'You will supply the mouse and we will watch over it and I promise you that it will reincarnate into another being or I will eat my hat.'

'Looks like you've eaten it already,' said Cubby, poking Cecil playfully in the stomach. 'Cor! It must have been a big'n by the feel of it.'

'It's just gas . . . Don't touch me! Step away!' yelled Cecil.

Cubby took a few steps back.

'Further!' said Cecil, flapping, but Cubby stepped forward again. He had a question he needed to ask.

'Sir Cecil, you know this dead mouse? What if it turns into a dog? Only you're scared of them, aren't you?

When you saw the duchess's chihuahua the other day, you had a little accident on the carpet.'

'That was nothing to do with the chihuahua,' bluffed Cecil. 'I was very ill at the time – a victim of Mrs Dortmunder's cooking.'

'But say the mouse comes back as a Rottweiler?' continued Cubby.

'As my assistant, it'll be your job to scare it away,' said Cecil. 'I won't be able to, because I'll be too busy taking notes.'

Cubby was so certain the experiment wouldn't work he decided to go along with it anyway, just for a laugh. 'I'll go and get the mouse then, shall I?' he said. 'Any particular colour?'

'No, no,' said Cecil, 'but it's got to be a whole mouse. No snacking on the legs. The experiment won't work unless it's a perfect specimen. Bring it to the drawing room. I'll be under the grand piano. Now run along, Mr Cubs. I haven't got all day.'

While Cubby was out in the grounds of Futtock Mansion hunting down the mouse, Cecil bumbled lazily into the kitchen and ate his way through some of the excellent hamper that Mrs Dortmunder had left earlier. There were trout fillets, quail eggs and potted cheese. It all looked so good, it was hard to know where to start. It was even harder to know when to stop, so he didn't. He ate until his belly touched the floor. It was all he could do to drag his saggy self to the drawing room, and a miracle that he fitted under the piano at all. When he arrived, Cubby was already waiting for him with the dead mouse.

'I don't know how you can put that dirty thing in your mouth,' grimaced Cecil, who had never hunted for anything more lively than a custard cream.

'Where were you, Sir Cecil, sir?' asked Cubby. 'I've been waiting ages.'

'Me? Oh, I was doing a bit of

research,' he replied. 'Someone has to do it.'

'Did it involve potted cheese?' wondered Cubby. 'There's some in your eyebrows.'

'It's a skin condition,' blustered Cecil. 'Enough banter, let's get on, shall we?'

Cubby dropped the dead mouse on the priceless Persian rug and waited for instructions.

'We'll take it in turns to watch,' said Cecil, yawning loudly. 'You can go first and, whatever you do, don't leave the room – is that clear? Or I'll have Master Hooray shoot you with his spud gun.'

'Whatever,' said Cubby, 'but I thought you were going to take notes. Where's your pen?'

'How the fiddling fox am I supposed to hold a pen?' spluttered Sir Cecil. 'When I come back as a person, *then* I'll take notes with a pen because I'll have proper thumbs, but until that day – hopefully tomorrow – I shall be taking *mental* notes, if that's all right with you.'

Cubby peeled his eyes open and gazed at the dead mouse. It was a nice plump one and as the minutes ticked by he found it harder and harder not to pounce on it. Cecil was asleep; he could easily nip over and eat it – but how to explain the missing body? Maybe he could say that the mouse turned into a wasp and flew out of the window, but then Cecil would think the experiment had worked. He'd be an even more unbearable know-it-all and insist on being killed all over again. Cubby didn't need the hassle.

He left his post and went out into the garden in search of a shrew to snack on. He guessed there would be nothing left in the hamper Mrs Dortmunder had provided, and as he went out through the cat flap in the kitchen he could tell by the trail of trout juice, egg yolk and cheese crumbs that Cecil had scoffed the lot.

Three shrews later, he came back.

He was pretty certain Cecil would still be asleep – indeed he could hear him snoring like a beast from the kitchen. But as he approached the drawing room his ears pricked up – there was another sound coming from in there – a high-pitched gurgling as if someone had beaten him to it and was strangling Cecil. He pushed the door open cautiously and looked in.

His ginger eyes grew wider and wider. There, sitting in a carry seat exactly where the mouse had been, was a baby waving a teddy and cooing. Cubby crept up and felt under the seat – there

was no mouse! It had definitely gone – or had it?

Could the mouse have changed into a baby while he was off hunting for shrews? Cubby might not have been to boarding school but he was no fool. Mice didn't just turn into babies – not that quickly anyway. The more he looked at the infant, the more it looked like a small version of Mrs Dortmunder, only smoother; it was probably her grandson.

Although Mrs Dortmunder wasn't

due to return until Cecil's dinnertime, she must have come back to Futtock Mansion early for whatever reason – a sneaky session in the Jacuzzi perhaps, while the Hoorays were away. She'd left the baby in the drawing room, at which point she would have spotted the dead mouse and thrown it away. Cubby was about to go and check in the dustbin when suddenly Cecil woke up and saw the baby.

'Whoo hoo! What did I tell you, Mr Cubs?' he whooped. 'It worked!'

Cubby sighed inwardly – should he go and find the dead mouse and prove Cecil wrong?

'Don't you see?' said Cecil gleefully, circling the carry seat. 'If a mouse can come back as a baby, a cat of my pedigree can surely come back as a king!'

Cubby was about to explain that the baby was probably just a relative of Mrs Dortmunder's, but Cecil was far too excited to listen to reason.

'Tell me what I missed, Mr Cubs.

Spare me no details. When the mouse reincarnated, were there flashing lights? The sound of angels trumpeting?'

'N– Oh yes! Angels trumping,' said Cubby. 'And flashing like you wouldn't believe.' He realized that if he didn't make up something on the spot and describe it all in detail, Cecil would know he'd left his post and instruct Young Master Hooray to shoot him with his spud gun. While being peppered with bits of raw potato wasn't going to kill him, Cubby didn't fancy spending the whole of the Easter holidays as a moving target for that dreadful boy.

So he lied. He pretended the experiment had worked.

3

'If you refuse to kill me, I shall just have to kill myself, Mr Cubs,' announced Cecil, mincing up the spiral staircase in the bell tower. Cubby hurried after him, feeling guilty for pretending that the dead mouse had changed into a baby and hoping he could persuade Cecil from jumping out of the window. There were two reasons for this: 1. If Cecil was no more, there would be no more top nosh. 2. He'd grown fond of the old fur bag.

'Don't do it, Sir Cecil, sir!' he said. 'Don't jump!'

'Why not? Why wait a moment longer to fulfill my dream of becoming the puff . . . the puff . . . the puf . . . ect person?' puffed Cecil.

He had very short legs, the stairs were steep and there were too many of them for his liking.

'It's an awful long way down, Sir Cecil,' said Cubby. 'You'll make a rotten mess when you hit the deck. Think of poor Mrs Dortmunder having to scrape you off the patio.'

They reached the top and Cecil pushed him aside. He pulled himself up on to the window sill.

'Out of my way, Mr Cubs! Help me get this window open – I'm all paws and claws.'

'But, Sir Cecil, what if you come back as a monkey?'

'You'll see!' he cried, and before Cubby could stop him Cecil had elbowed the stiff window catch, climbed out on to the ledge and hurled himself off with a fat smile on his face.

'Farewell, Mr Cuuuuuuuuu . . .'

Cubby closed his eyes and waited for the splat. He waited and waited. It was a very high bell tower, but even though Cubby had never had a physics lesson he was pretty sure that something as heavy as Cecil should have landed ages ago. He took a deep breath and peered out of the window.

Down below, he could see the stable block where Young Master Hooray kept his polo ponies. In the stable block was a huge steaming pile of horse manure and in the middle of the pile of horse manure there was something that looked like a sticky brown beaver kicking its legs in the air. Cubby raced back down the stairs and out into the yard.

'Is that *you*, Sir Cecil?' he called up.

'Only, if it is, I'm afraid you've reincarnated into something you didn't want to – a beaver or possibly a pygmy hippopotamus.'

'Just shut up! Shut up and pull me out,' wailed Cecil. 'I'm sinking!'

'You're stinking, you mean,' said Cubby. 'Give me your paw, sir. That's it, and the other one . . . one, two, three, heave!'

There was a loud plop and Cecil slid down the steep, smelly heap on to the cobbles below.

'If I were you, I'd give myself a scrub in the horse trough and forget all about this crazy plan, sir,' said Cubby.

'Yes, but you are not me!' said Cecil. 'The fact that *I* am still me is just . . . a blip . . . a trial run. Next time, I shall succeed, Mr Cubs. I *shall* become a person. Now, excuse me while I throw myself down the wishing well.'

'Well, I wish you wouldn't,' said Cubby, following downwind of smelly Cecil. 'You'll miss *Antiques in the Attic*, sir. It's your favourite programme.'

Cecil turned round and beamed at him. 'I shan't miss it at all. I shan't miss it, because I shall be able to watch it through new eyes – *human* eyes! I shouldn't take very long to drown in the well and we have scientific proof that reincarnation only takes a jiffy – the adverts will still be on by the time I'm done.'

With that, Cecil ran out of the stable yard towards the orchard where there was a very deep, very ancient well that used to supply Futtock Mansion with spring water.

'I do hope you're a good swimmer,' said Cubby as Cecil gathered speed.

'I don't want to swim; I want to

drown, Mr Cubs!' he blustered. 'Let go of my tail. I shall now take a running jump . . .'

'My old mum always used to say "Look before you leap",' warned Cubby, but it was too late. Cecil had leapt over the well wall and gone straight down the hole with a very loud, very long *mi-aaaaaaagh*!

Cubby waited for the splash. He waited and waited but it didn't come and even though he'd never had a lesson in weights and measures, he knew that something as porky as Cecil should have hit the water by now.

He tiptoed to the edge of the well and looked down. To his surprise, there was only about ten centimetres of stagnant-looking water in the well and right at the bottom, wedged tightly in a rusty bucket on a chain, there appeared to be a burst pillow covered in green slime.

'Wind me back up!' it wailed.

Cubby wound the handle. It wasn't easy with paws and the bucket clanked and the chain squeaked and the green slimy pillow kept grumbling and swearing.

'Oh, it's *you* again, Sir Cecil, sir!' said Cubby as the bucket finally came to the top. 'I am pleased. I thought for a terrible minute you'd turned into some old bedding – did you know there's a frog on your head?'

'Of course I know!' snapped Cecil. 'All the best cats are wearing frogs on their heads this season, Mr Cubs. Don't you know anything about fashion?'

'I don't know much about hats,' said Cubby, 'but I know everything there is to know about knickers, which is what comes of being born and bred under a knicker stall in the market. There are French knickers, full briefs, bikini pants and boxers. Woolly ones, frilly ones, sensible and silly ones . . . Why are you pulling that funny face, sir?'

'Your knicker knowledge is not helping me one bit!' exploded Cecil.

'All right, no need to get yours in a

twist, sir,' said Cubby. 'What's up? Are you stuck in that bucket or are you just having a nice sit-down?'

'Get me out!' wailed Cecil. 'I think I'm sitting on a slug.'

After much heaving and pulling and yowling, Cecil was unwedged, but he looked so sorry for himself Cubby wasn't sure what to say for the best.

'Would it cheer you up if we had a sing-song, sir?' he asked. 'Or I could show you my little tap-dance routine, if you like. The one I learned from the one-eyed busker?'

'I'd rather roast my own head,' groaned Cecil. Suddenly his eyes lit up. 'That's it!' he cried. 'Death by cooking! I'll climb into Mrs Dortmunder's oven, you turn it on and bingo!'

'That's not bingo,' said Cubby. 'Bingo's a game where you have to match the number on the balls to the ones on your card, sir. There was a bingo hall in the market where I was born and bre–'

'Never mind that. How long do you think I'd take to cook?' interrupted Cecil.

Cubby, who'd never had a cookery lesson in his life, looked Cecil up and down. He'd listened to the man who sold poultry in the market on many occasions and he guessed that Cecil weighed about two turkeys.

'It takes the best part of Christmas morning to cook a big turkey, sir, so I reckon we'd have to put you in the oven until Boxing Day at the earliest.'

'Hmmm . . . that's far too long,' sighed Cecil. 'I was hoping to be reincarnated by the end of this afternoon. I need to think of a quicker way.'

'No, you don't,' said Cubby. 'You need to go back into the mansion and live out the rest of your nine lives in peace like a good pussycat, sir. Being human isn't all it's cracked up to be. Young Master Hooray is what they call a hoodlum, sir. He's the devil in short trousers. I've seen his photo in the drawing room – Why would you want to be like him?'

'Why on earth would I want to be you, Mr Cubs?' grumbled Sir Cecil. 'You may think it's perfectly acceptable to cough up fur balls and poop in plant pots and eat rodents, but I do not. I want to sit at the table in a suit and tie and eat from a china plate.'

Cubby shook his head in despair. 'Isn't there nuffin' you like about being a cat, Sir Cecil?'

Cecil thought for a moment. He was clearly struggling. 'I quite like eating string,' he said, 'but then so does Young Master Hooray.'

'String, sir? I can find you some string,' said Cubby. 'I know where there's a great big ball of it.'

'Excellent. You can strangle me with it!' said Cecil.

'Ooh no, sir. It's very cheap string,' said Cubby hastily. 'It'll only snap and you'll be so disappointed. Let's go in and watch your nice antique show instead, shall we, sir?'

'Oh, very well. If you insist,'

muttered Cecil. Cubby hadn't expected Cecil to do as he suggested and was very pleased that for once, he'd listened to him. But he wasn't pleased for long. Just as he was halfway through the cat flap, Cecil did a bunk and went running down the gravel drive and out on to the pavement. Cubby raced after him.

'That's the wrong way, Sir Cecil, sir!'

'No, Mr Cubs. It's the only way.'

'Come back, Sir Cecil!' called Cubby. 'You'll get run over.'

Cecil took no notice. He sat down,

right in the middle of the road, and waited.

And waited and waited and waited. There wasn't a car in sight. Or a lorry. Or a bike. There wasn't even a doll's pram.

'What's going on, Mr Cubs? Where's all the traffic?' whined Cecil.

'The road's been closed off due to gas works,' said Cubby. 'Expect delays for another fortnight.'

'A *fortnight*?' wailed Cecil. 'But that's . . . eighteen days!'

Cubby had never had a maths lesson in his life, but he knew the price of pants and how to add up and how many days there were until market day because he'd been born and bred in one.

'I think you'll find a fortnight is only fourteen days, Sir Cecil.'

'Not according to Young Master Hooray's maths tutor, it isn't!' groaned Cecil. 'And he's very well educated, but even if it was fourteen that's still . . . er . . . um . . . thirteen days too many!'

'Come out of the road, Sir Cecil. You'll get all gritty sitting there.'

'But I want to die,' wailed Cecil, beating his chest with his own paws.

'And so you will, but not until you're a dribbly old grandad cat with no teeth, sir,' said Cubby, dragging him on to the pavement and back into Futtock Mansion by his tail. But, no matter what he said, Cecil would not give up his quest for reincarnation and as he sat on the sofa mournfully watching *Antiques in the Attic*, he came up with more and more ridiculous ways of ending it all.

'What if I stuck my head in the ceiling fan in the ballroom?'

'No, Sir Cecil.'

'All right then, shut me in the freezer.'

'Shan't, Sir Cecil.'

'Run me through with a toasting fork?'

'Nope . . . Oh, please don't cry, sir.'

But Cecil did cry, and he wouldn't stop crying until Cubby promised to give him a killing bite, such as a lion might give to a goat, and leave him to die in his basket.

'You'll be doing me a huge kindness,

Mr Cubs,' he insisted. 'When I come back as a person, I shall repay you handsomely. Just think! I'll be able to use a tin opener. I'll open as many tins of cat food as you can eat.'

Finally, Cubby gave in.

'Oh, all right, then,' he said. 'I'll give it a go, but I'm not sure I'll be able to kill you. You've got a very chubby neck, if you don't mind me saying so, Sir Cecil. I'm not sure my fangs are long enough to get through all that flab.'

Cecil rolled on to his back, lifted

his many chins and exposed his fluffy throat.

'Just do it, Mr Cubs.'

Reluctantly, Cubby got ready to pounce.

'Here I come, Sir Cecil. Brace yourself, sir!'

Cubby leapt on to his furry friend, but he tasted so disgusting, what with the manure and the slime, he just gave him a few harmless nips in the hope that it would be enough to make Cecil change his mind, but it didn't.

'Ha, ha, that tickles, Mr Cubs! That's useless . . . hee hee . . . Put your back into it!'

Cubby seized him by the scruff and was so busy rolling Cecil around the floor he didn't see Mrs Dortmunder creep up. And when she whacked him on the bottom with her broom he was so surprised he accidentally sank his teeth into Cecil's head.

'Mi . . . *ow*!' screamed Cecil. 'That . . . was . . . the . . . one, Mr Cubs. Now . . . I . . . die!'

He shuddered and closed his eyes, but before Cubby could check Cecil's pulse Mrs Dortmunder booted him out of the back door and locked the cat flap.

4

Night fell. There was still no sign of Cecil and all the lights were out. Cubby pressed his nose to the cat flap and peered in hopefully, but he was not in the kitchen. Even more worrying, Mrs Dortmunder hadn't come back to refresh the hamper and it was way past teatime.

Was Cecil dead or alive? Cubby didn't know, but he had to find out. There was only one thing for it. He would have to get back inside Futtock Mansion somehow and see if he could find him.

The cat flap was still locked and, unfortunately, Mrs Dortmunder was very hot on security. She had locked all the windows and doors as well before she'd left. There was only one way in as far as Cubby could see and that was down the crooked chimney above the drawing room.

In order to get to the chimney, he needed to climb up the monkey puzzle tree, which was almost the same height as the roof. This wasn't too difficult, but the distance from the tree to the edge of the gutter was much further than it looked from down below. Cubby wondered what would happen if he fell. A cat usually lands on its feet, but it would be unlikely for even the luckiest cat to survive a fall from that great height.

He crept along the branch nearest to

the gutter and clung on for dear life – but then he thought to himself, *Well, if I die, so what? Cecil might be right. I could come back as a leopard and stalk Young Master Hooray and Sir Cecil all around the grounds and scare the wits out of them.*

With that happy thought, Cubby got the branch bouncing and catapulted himself through the air in the general direction of the roof. To his enormous relief, his front claws caught in some ivy that was clinging even harder to the tiles than he was.

Cubby inched himself along on his belly by hooking on to the thick, twisted stems until he reached the chimney pot.

There was an old birds' nest on top of it, which meant the chimney hadn't been swept and the flue was bound to be caked in soot.

Cubby knocked the birds' nest away and stared down the hole. The brickwork inside was higgledy piggledy and, as he lowered himself in tail first, he was able to feel around with his toes for bits of sticking-out brick that he could use as steps.

Using this technique, he was able to climb all the way down except for the last four metres where, for some reason, the chimney lining became smooth. Suddenly his paws lost their grip and he fell with an undignified clatter into the grate, only to be greeted by a scream of terror. Cubby rubbed the soot out of his eyes to see who it was.

'Ooh, is that *you,* Sir Cecil, sir?'

Cowering behind the leather chair was a tubby little man wearing a balaclava, not unlike the one Master Hooray wore when he went skiing in the Alps. Cubby couldn't help noticing that the man had a shock of white hair poking out of the front, identical to the colour of Cecil's fur. He also had very similar blue eyes.

In fact, the man hiding behind the chair looked so much like Cecil would have done if he'd shaved and put on a pair of baggy tracksuit bottoms that Cubby needed no more convincing. He sidled over and stuck a friendly claw into the gentleman's buttock for old time's sake.

The man whipped round and glared at him.

'It's all right, Sir Cecil!' said Cubby. 'It's only me. I don't suppose you recognize me all covered in soot. I expect you thought I was that vicious black tom who attacked you that time you fell asleep in the rhubarb patch.'

The man peered at Cubby and a look of relief spread over what could be seen of his face behind the knitted balaclava.

'Phew – just a little moggy. Blimey, I thought I was done for. You scared the life out of me, you little tinker!'

Cubby was amazed that Cecil had grasped the gift of human speech so swiftly.

'You scared the life out of me too, Sir Cecil!' he said. 'I thought I'd gone and killed you when I didn't see you in the kitchen – I never meant to do it, it was the shock of those bristles in Mrs Dortmunder's broom.'

The man smiled broadly and patted Cubby on the head.

'There's a good puss,' he said.

It seemed that Sir Cecil was delighted

to be alive in his new form, even though he was more like the man who used to sweep up at the market than a soul mate for Young Master Hooray. Cubby watched as he picked up the carriage clock on the mantelpiece and examined it.

'Sorry I scared you just now, Sir Cecil,' chirped Cubby. 'I expect you thought I was Young Master Hooray come home early for his holidays. I expect when I dropped down the chimney just now you thought it was him playing a prank, sir.'

The man put the clock back down.

'Fake,' he grunted.

'Well, you always said that clock wasn't the real thing, didn't you, sir? Ever since we saw the genuine article on your antiques programme.'

'You don't half miaow a lot, don't you?' said the man, who began searching through the oak writing bureau.

'I do miaow,' said Cubby, 'and so did you till very recently, don't you remember?'

Clearly he didn't because the man

just looked at him blankly, took a large wad of money out of an envelope he'd found in one of the drawers and stuffed it in his jacket pocket.

'That'll do nicely,' he said.

'I expect you'll be needing that to buy a smart suit and some elocution lessons,' said Cubby. 'You do look a bit scruffy, sir, and you sound frightful common. I'm not sure Young Master Hooray will want to hang around with you, looking and sounding like you do.'

The man unplugged the television and carried it over to the window, which he'd unlocked earlier with a crowbar. Just then, a van drew up. The driver got out, took the TV from the man in the balaclava and loaded it into the van. Cubby couldn't imagine why Cecil would give his television away – it was one of his favourite things.

'Sir Cecil, why are you giving that man our telly?'

Then it dawned on him.

'Are you thinking of getting one with an even wider screen? Good idea!'

The man climbed out of the window.

'Don't you tell nobody it was me, all right, pussy cat?'

'All right, Sir Cecil. I won't tell a soul. It'll be our little secret. Shall I see you when you've had a bath and smartened yourself up, sir? I was going to say meet me in the kitchen by your food bowl, but I expect you'll want your dinner sitting at the table in your bow tie.'

The man winked at Cubby, pushed the window shut and hurried down the path. Cubby watched as he got into the van and was driven off. When they'd gone, he settled down on the sofa to have a sleep. Then he heard the familiar throbbing of Mrs Dortmunder's 1,000cc motorbike crunching to a halt on the gravel drive.

He jumped down and ran into the hall and found her bow-legged under the weight of an enormous cardboard box done up with string. He seriously hoped it was food. Whatever was in it must have weighed a ton if an ex-Olympic shot-putter like Mrs Dortmunder was struggling to carry it.

She groaned as she put the box down on the floor and rubbed her back. As she unzipped her leather biker gloves, Cubby noticed that her hands were covered in fresh scratches.

He thought at first that she'd got them wrestling, because, despite her age, she still liked a good grapple in the ring, but then something changed his mind – the box began to growl. There was something alive inside and although Cubby had never had a biology lesson in his life he suspected it wasn't a chicken.

Suddenly a white paw shot out through one of the cardboard flaps like a surrender flag.

'Is that *you*, Sir Cecil, sir?' exclaimed Cubby. 'Whatever are you doing in there, sir? I thought you'd come back as a man.'

'Noooooooo!' screeched Sir Cecil, bursting out of the box as Mrs Dortmunder bit through the string. 'I have come back from the v– from the v–'

'Oh no, not the vet's?' said Cubby, noting the bald patch on his head where the vet had shaved round the bite wound.

'Look what he did to me!' wailed Cecil. 'I look ridiculous.'

'You, sir? Never,' said Cubby, trying very hard not to laugh. 'It'll grow back, and in the meantime you could always place a frog over it. It's all the rage, I believe.'

Cecil hid behind the curtain and refused to come out, so Cubby went and joined him.

'I'm sorry I didn't finish you off

good and proper, sir,' he said apologetically, but to his astonishment Cecil wasn't blaming him at all. He even went as far as praising him – the person he was furious with was the housekeeper.

'You did your best, Mr Cubs. There I was bleeding to death perfectly happily on top of Master Hooray's Spider-Man duvet when along came Mrs Dortmunder and bundled me off. I tried to fight her, but, as you know, she has a black belt in origami.'

'You didn't stand a chance, Sir Cecil,' said Cubby sympathetically. 'Are you definitely going to live now? I hope so, because we do have a laugh, don't we, sir?'

'Laugh? I may die of shame,' wailed Cecil. 'Mind you, I don't suppose Master Hooray would even notice if I was gone,' he added sadly. 'He never wanted me to be a cat, you know. He wanted a polar bear.'

'Well, *I* want you to be a cat,' said Cubby fondly. 'There's no shame in being a cat, sir. Not even one like you.'

Sir Cecil – who'd never had a real friend – was extremely touched that Cubby wanted him to stay as he was, and though he could hardly bear to admit it even to himself he was secretly warming to him. Things had been much more fun since Cubby had arrived. Maybe being a cat wasn't so bad after all.

'I don't think I'll bother with reincarnation for a while,' mumbled

Cecil. 'It's awfully hard work. Birtwhistle might have had the decency to point that out. I've a good mind never to watch him again.'

'You might never watch anything again,' confessed Cubby. 'While you were at the vet's, there was a man in the drawing room. I thought it was you, come back as a person, but on hindsight I think he may have been a tea leaf, sir.'

Cecil's eyebrows knitted in confusion.

'A *tea* leaf?'

'It's cockney rhyming slang for "thief", sir,' explained Cubby.

'Really? What makes you think he was burgling the place?' asked Cecil.

'Little things gave it away, sir. Like the way he stole the telly.'

As if to confirm it, somebody in the drawing room let out a deep bark like an elephant seal. It was Mrs Dortmunder. She'd just realized that the window had been jemmied and the money and the television had gone. Within minutes, there were policemen swarming all over Futtock Mansion and Cecil had one of his panic attacks.

'Come on, sir,' said Cubby, 'let's hide under the bureau. The boys in blue won't bother us there. Breathe in and you should be able to squeeze under . . . That's the way.'

'I'm so fed up, Mr Cubs,' whimpered Cecil. 'Just as I try to come to terms with being a cat, suddenly I'm a cat without a television. Tell me things can't get any worse!'

The chief inspector came into the drawing room.

'It doesn't matter how well you lock up, Mrs Dortmunder,' he said. 'If a burglar wants to get in, he will. If I was you, I'd get a couple of guard dogs.'

'Things just got worse, sir,' whispered Cubby.

'A c-c-couple of guard dogs?' stammered Cecil. 'Over my dead body!'

Suddenly his expression changed.

He smiled so broadly his whiskers stuck out like aerials.

'Oh . . . *yes*! If there were guard dogs, they'd rip me to shreds in an instant. I'd be far too dead to be taken to the vet's, wouldn't I, Mr Cubs? I do hope they arrive today. I could come back as a gentleman before the shops shut and buy a new TV. Mrs Dortmunder? Fetch me some Dobermanns this instant!'

'Oh no. Don't start that again, sir,' sighed Cubby. He decided he was going to have to put a stop to it all. The threat of Young Master Hooray shooting him with spuds was no way to live, but he couldn't let Cecil go to the dogs.

'Sir Cecil, you know that dead mouse?' he blurted. 'It never really reincarnated into a baby. Mrs Dortmunder picked it up and chucked it in the bin.'

Cecil patted him on the head and smiled. 'Nonsense, you saw it with your own eyes – there was trumpeting and flashing. You just don't want me to come back as a person. I believe you're a teeny bit jealous, Mr Cubs.'

Cubby took a deep breath.

'I didn't see nuffin' of the sort. I . . . left . . . my . . . post,' he confessed, inching out from under the bureau. Cecil narrowed his eyes and, when the truth finally sank in, it was amazing how fast such a fat cat could chase a skinny one all around Futtock Mansion.

'Just you wait! I'll have you shot!' he screeched as Cubby swung on the chandelier in the ballroom.

But even though Cubby had never been to boarding school he'd had lots of lessons in Cecilology and he knew that, despite their enormous differences, they were going to be friends for life.

Psssssssssssst!
If you love Puffin Books
you should choose
There's nuffin' like a Puffin!
Est. 2008
Puffin Post
Here's what's in it for you:
6 magazines
6 free books a year (of your choice)
The chance to see YOUR writing in print
PLUS
Exclusive author features
Articles
Quizzes
Competitions and games
And that's not all.
You get PRESENTS too.
Simply subscribe here to become a member
puffinpost.co.uk
and wait for your copy to decorate your doorstep.
(WARNING – reading Puffin Post may make you late for school.)

It all started with a Scarecrow.

Puffin is seventy years old.

Sounds ancient, doesn't it? But Puffin has never been so lively. We're always on the lookout for the next big idea, which is how it began all those years ago.

Penguin Books was a big idea from the mind of a man called Allen Lane, who in 1935 invented the quality paperback and changed the world.

And from great Penguins, great Puffins grew, changing the face of children's books forever.

The first four Puffin Picture Books were hatched in 1940 and the first Puffin story book featured a man with broomstick arms called Worzel Gummidge. In 1967 Kaye Webb, Puffin Editor, started the Puffin Club, promising to **'make children into readers'**. She kept that promise and over 200,000 children became devoted Puffineers through their quarterly instalments of *Puffin Post*, which is now back for a new generation.

Many years from now, we hope you'll look back and remember Puffin with a smile. **No matter what your age or what you're into, there's a Puffin for everyone.** The possibilities are endless, but one thing is for sure: whether it's a picture book or a paperback, a sticker book or a hardback, **if it's got that little Puffin on it – it's bound to be good.**